This book belongs to

....

....

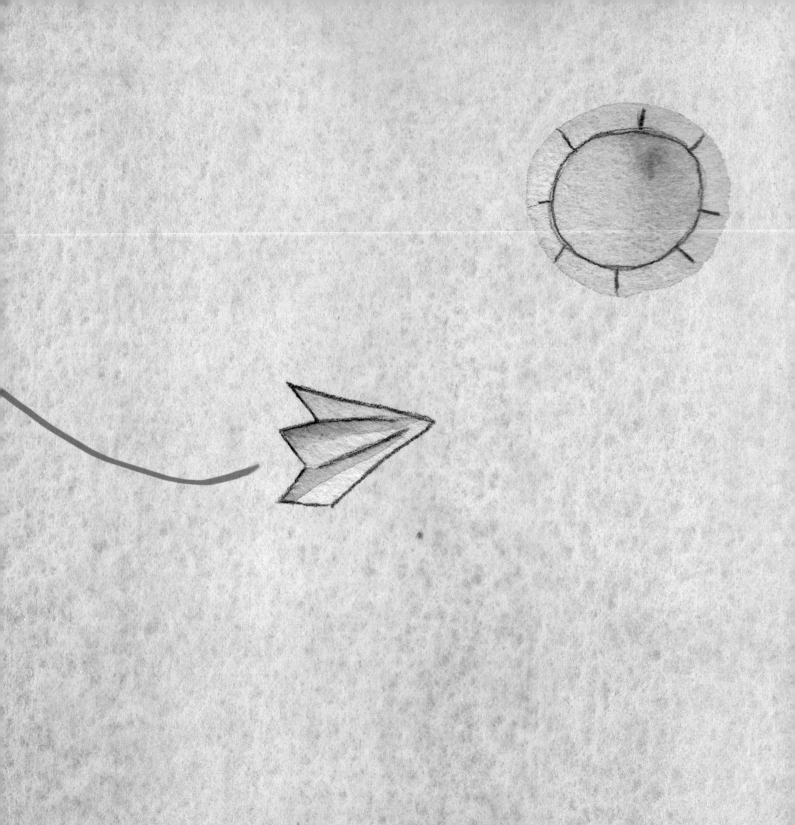

For Nic
- L.P.

This edition first published in 2018 by Alligator Products Ltd.
Cupcake is an imprint of Alligator Products Ltd.
2nd Floor, 314 Regents Park Road, London N3 2JX

Written by Leyland Perree
Illustrated by Joelle Dreidemy

ISBN: 978-1-84750-709-9

Printed in China.0793

The GOAT that GLOATS

cupcake

On a throne made of stone at the top of a tower
Counting the minutes of each passing hour,
Feeling bored and ignored for days without end
Lived a goat who was lonely; he wanted a friend.

This goat was unhappy with sitting alone
Way up in his tower on his cold, hard throne,
So out of his window he started to bleat
To the people who bustled below in the street.

'What a **wonderful** friend I would make!'
bragged the goat.
'I've a thr**One** in a tower with a **bubble-bath** moat.'

But the people below called back over the moat,
'Who'd **want** to be friends with a gloating goat?'

The goat scratched his head with his hoof, and he frowned.
What must he do to make friends in this town?
So he shouted again to the people below
Without even so much as a smile or hello.

'What a **wonderful** friend I would make!'
bragged the goat.
'For I own a **fast** car and a **fabulous** boat!'

But the people below called back over the moat,
'Who'd **want** to be friends with a gloating goat?'

Now the goat was beginning to get **quite** upset
That **no one** would want to be friends with him yet.
So he jumped to his hoofs and reached for his net,
And quickly he scooped up Fernando, his pet.

What a **wonderful** friend I would make!'
bragged the goat.
'For Fernando, my pet, is the world's **smartest** stoat!'
But the people below called back over the moat,

Who'd **want** to be friends with a gloating goat?'

Once more, the goat, who was **stricken** with grief
Came away from the window (to Fernando's relief)
He re-caged his pet before he got bitten.
Then **burst** into verse with a song that he'd written.

'What a **wonderful** friend I would make!'
bragged the goat.

'For that little **ditty** was one that I wrote!'

But the people below called back over the moat,
'Who'd **want** to be friends with a gloating goat?'

Now the goat was **about** to sing one more verse
But his run of **bad** luck took a turn for the worse.
He took a deep breath and let **loose** with such force
That his voice gave right out –
he had **bragged** himself **hoarse!**

The people below in the street clapped and cheered,
And the goat whimpered miserably into his beard,
Why don't they **like** me? Why don't they **care**?
When **all** of my riches I'm willing to **share**?

Meanwhile, the people began to feel bad
For **teasing** the goat in the way that they had.
He might be annoying for gloating all day.
But all that aside – he was kind of **okay**.

So they lifted their heads to the tower and they tried
To talk to the goat who was holed up inside
For they thought that he'd make a good friend, sure enough,
If only he'd promise to **stop showing off.**

The goat heard them calling his name and he jumped
Up out of his throne with such **JOY** that he bumped
His horns on a beam jutting out of the ceiling.
(It was **several** hours before they regained feeling).

But he couldn't talk with that pain in his throat.
He struggled to utter much more than a note.
A note? – Why, that's it! So he went one step better,
Sat down at his desk and he wrote them a letter.

At **last** he had finished. To the window he went
And there, with his letter, he carefully bent
And folded the paper to form a small plane
(Whilst all the time hoping that it **wouldn't** rain).

Whizz!

Went the letter out into the blue.
'Ahhh!' went the people below (also 'Oooh!')
As circling steadily over the street
It finally came to a rest at their feet.

"What wonderful friends you would make,"
went the note,
"For this foolish old goat
(with a very sore throat).

I am sorry, I really did not mean to brag.
But loneliness can be a terrible drag.

Now, I got to thinking, sat here on my chair,
What use are nice things if they cannot be shared?

I would take great delight in knowing you better

And that is the reason I'm sending this letter."

And the people below called back over the moat,
'Of course we'll be friends with you, silly old goat!'